W9-BMN-796

Niles and Bradford

Soccer Kicks

By: Marcy Blesy

This book is a work of fiction. Names, characters, places, and events are a result of the imagination of the author or are used fictitiously. Any resemblance to actual persons, living or dead, businesses, events, or locations is a coincidence.

No part of the text may be reproduced without the written permission of the author, except for brief passages in reviews.

Copyright © 2019 by Marcy Blesy. All rights reserved.

Cover design by Cormar Covers

Follow my blog for information about upcoming books or short stories.

Chapter 1:

Being not-the-new kid anymore makes Niles happy. He has a good group of friends. He has tried some new sports. Even with winter approaching, there is still stuff to do. Indoor soccer tryouts at the local community center are soon. There are only two things that Niles feels like he can count on when it comes to trying a new sport. One thing he knows is that he is not afraid to try something new. He works hard. Sometimes the hard work pays off, and he does well. He scores a goal. He makes a basket. He gets a hole in one. Sometimes he works hard and doesn't do well, but he likes playing either way.

The other thing Niles can count on is his best friend Bradford. Bradford is Niles's pet dragon. Bradford is not an imaginary friend. He's very much a real, orange, foot tall dragon. He is so good at staying hidden that no one has seen him except for Niles. That includes Niles's mom and dad and big sister Nora. There have been close calls—like the one time that Dad came into Niles's bedroom in the middle of the night when he heard a loud noise. Niles didn't know it, but Bradford had crawled into bed with him. He later told Niles he had had a bad dream about a giant bird hunting dragons. When Bradford sleeps, he snores—loud. Usually, no one can hear him because he sleeps in a pair of Niles's red fuzzy socks in his drawer. Red is his favorite color. But the night he had a dream, there he was snoring loudly on Niles's pillow. When dragons snore, they sound like a cannonball shooting out of a cannon. Booming. Loud. Niles sleeps through most things, so Dad heard the noise first. He flicked on the bedroom light.

"Niles, are you okay?" he asked.

Niles threw his arms in the air and opened his eyes widely when the light came on. When he did that, he sent Bradford flying across the bed.

"What on Earth?" said Dad.

Niles was awake then. So was Bradford. He *poofed* back into the sock drawer, hoping he had not been spotted.

It took a lot of talking by Niles to convince his dad that what he had seen was his Teenage Mutant Ninja Turtle stuffed animal flying across the bed and not a mutant-looking animal from another planet. That's how Dad had described Bradford.

Thankfully, Niles's Dad doesn't remember things well when he is super sleepy. He never brought up seeing an orange dragon in Niles's bed ever again.

There would be other close calls with Bradford. But so far, he's Niles's special secret.

Niles is ready for soccer tryouts tomorrow. Nothing can stand in his way.

Chapter 2:

Nora is trying out for soccer, too. She is older. The twelve-year-old team tries out first, so Mom makes Niles come, too. The nine-year-olds try out last. Niles kicks a soccer ball in the hallway practicing his footwork. That's what Nora calls it. Niles thinks it sounds cool—*footwork*. Niles tries extra hard to stay on his feet and not trip over the ball. There is probably more to *footwork* than that.

"Can I play, too?" A loud voice echoes off the walls. It surprises Niles. He turns around.

"Oh, *hello*, Della. Are there cheerleading tryouts today, too?" Niles asks.

Della punches Niles in the arm. "That's so rude, Niles Woodson. Girls can do other things besides cheerleading." Her curly red hair bounces up and down as she yells.

Niles looks surprised again. "I know that. I did not mean to make you mad. I just know that you were a cheerleader during my basketball games."

Della smiles. "You are right. I forgot you were not here last year. You did not know I am the best soccer player, too."

"That's cool," says Niles.

"Are you any good?"

"Um, I don't know."

"What do you mean?"

"I have never played before. Well, I *have* played soccer before but never on a team." Niles wants to ask a question but decides he had better not.

"I need to practice my goal kicks on the practice field. Maybe you should keep practicing, too." Della flips the soccer ball up in the air. It hits Niles in the shoulder and rolls back to the floor. He watches Della run to the practice field.

"She's dreamy," says a soft voice inside Niles's bag. The zipper is open at the top.

"Bradford, she brags too much," says Niles.

Bradford shakes his little orange tail. "That red hair...that...red...hair."

Bradford loves anything that is red. Of course, he would like Della. Niles zips the bag up tight.

"Forget about Della," says Niles. "I need help. Let's go outside. You can pass me the ball with your tail if you stay behind my bag. Okay?"

"Really? I am on it. *On it!* But do I get extra peanut butter sandwiches tonight—*no jelly*? Because I will be working up a sweat, you know?"

"Yes, Bradford. You can have extra sandwiches. Just stay out of trouble. Got it?"

"And no crusts on the bread?"

"No crusts, Bradford."

Bradford unzips the bag from the inside again. He puts his little hand to his head and salutes Niles. "At your service."

Chapter 3:

Nora smiles when she sees Niles sitting in the bleachers at the end of her tryout. "Soccer is so awesome," she says.

Niles gives her a high five. For a sister, Nora is pretty cool. "I don't think I will make the team," he says.

"Of course, you will," she says. "You love sports."

"Just because I love sports doesn't mean I will make the team," says Niles.

"Do your best."

"You sound like Mom."

"Oh, man. Let's not go that far!"

Someone clears her throat behind them. For a second Niles thinks it is Bradford, but his bag is down by the field. He turns around.

"Hi, Mom." Niles and Nora share a laugh.

"Do your best and get out there." She points to the soccer field where a coach is calling names from a clipboard.

"Thanks." Niles gives his mom a quick hug and runs onto the field just as his name is called.

"I am Coach Beth. I am the co-ed soccer 9s coach this season." She doesn't smile. "I expect most of you will make the team. We need ten kids. There are twelve here."

"That would really stink to not make it," says Rashid. He doesn't smile, either. Rashid almost always smiles.

"Let's focus on our skills," says Coach Beth. "I will focus on team numbers. Okay?" She looks right at Rashid. He nods his head. If he were a turtle, he would have pulled his head right into his shell at that very moment.

The first thing the kids do is kick soccer balls between orange cones on the field. They are organized into two groups. They weave in and out, trying not to touch the cones. Rashid and Scotty follow Niles. Kyle and Nick lead the pack. In the second group, Della zips through the cones. She runs so far ahead that it looks like she is in a one-person group. But behind her are Otis, Connor, Vinnie, Maggie, Lila, and Kate.

The whistle blows. Everyone stops and looks at Coach Beth.

"You! You!"

Rashid looks at Scotty. Scotty looks at Kyle. Kyle looks at Connor. Then everyone looks at Niles. Coach Beth is staring at him.

"Where are your shin guards?" she asks Niles.

Niles looks down at his lower legs. "Sorry, Coach. They are in my bag." Niles points to his bag that is still sitting next to the field.

"Don't stand there! Go put them on. You cannot play soccer without safety. Safety first. Everyone repeat after me, *safety first!*"

Everyone repeats Coach Beth while Niles runs to the sidelines for his shin guards. He wishes he could keep running and not look back. He opens his bag. As soon as he does, a tiny hand grabs his wrist.

"That lady is *mean*," says Bradford. "*M-E-A-N, mean!*"

"*Shhh.* Just hand me my shin guards."

Bradford holds up the shin guards. "Stick with Della. She is amazing." If Bradford could have stars in his eyes, they would be shining bright right now.

"You only like her because she has red hair. She's about as friendly as Coach Beth." Niles kicks off his soccer cleats and socks. He pulls the shin guards over his feet and onto his ankles. They cover the bottom part of his legs. "Stay in here. Don't make any trouble. I have enough of that today." Niles zips up the bag and runs back to the field.

The players are paired up and kicking the soccer balls back and forth. Only one person does not have a partner.

"You and Della pair up," says Coach Beth. "Now that you are protected."

Niles thinks she might be laughing behind her clipboard, but he is not sure. Soon he finds out why she may have been giggling. Della kicks the ball so hard it stings his leg, even *under* the shin guard.

"Ouch!" Niles yells. But he does not give up. "Ouch!" he says again when Della kicks the ball.

"Use the inside of your foot!" yells Della. "Don't use your shin!" She kicks the ball again. "You have to *think,* Niles. Hey, what was that?"

Niles trips over the ball. He follows Della's finger that is pointing toward the banners that are hanging above the bleachers. *District 7 Champions 2018, Regional Champions 2014, Sectional Champions 2015, 2016.* Niles sees it, too. But as soon as he sees it, it disappears. He knows exactly what he sees. Della does not.

"I don't see anything," says Niles, crossing his fingers because he doesn't like to lie. But that little orange tail, even for a split second, has given him away. Bradford is hiding in the rafters behind the red *Sectional Champions* banner. Niles kicks the soccer ball back to Della. This time she is not prepared.

"Ouch!" she says.

"You have to be ready, Della," says Coach Beth as she walks by.

Della scrunches up her face. It is almost as red as her hair. Niles can't help but smile. Maybe bringing Bradford to tryouts wasn't such a bad idea after all.

Chapter 4:

"Why aren't you happy?" asks Bradford. He sits on top of Niles's soccer ball in his bedroom. But it is hard to balance on top of a ball. He wobbles back and forth, crashing into a floor lamp. Niles jumps up. He catches the lamp right before it falls to the ground.

"Bradford!" Niles yells a little too loud.

Bradford *poofs* under the bed. "Sorry," he says in a whisper.

Niles barely hears him. "I'm not mad, buddy," says Niles. "I wish I made the team."

Bradford *poofs* back to the bed. "You *did* make the team. What are you talking about?"

"I am only on the team because Coach Beth said *everyone* could be on the team. She did that because Kyle hurt his ankle. That only left one person who would be cut. That person would have been *me*."

"You don't know that," says Bradford. He hands Niles a tissue.

"Bradford, a tissue is not the answer to all problems," says Niles. But he takes the tissue anyway.

"Do you want a bandage? Sometimes your mom gives Nora a bandage when she cries."

"I am not crying!" Niles yells. "Sorry. I know you are trying to help me feel better."

"Do you know what helps me feel better?" Bradford draws an imaginary heart in the air.

Niles smiles. "Peanut butter and jelly?"

"Whhhaaa…" Bradford spits out a stream of smoke.

Niles waves away the smoke and laughs. "Just kidding. Peanut butter—no jelly?"

"Perfect. Yes." Bradford shakes his head up and down. "*Three sandwiches*—one for you and two for me."

Niles hopes that peanut butter, no jelly, will make him a better soccer player, too. But he is not so sure.

Chapter 5:

Niles puts on his Clearview 9s purple jersey. The first game is today. He pulls on his long socks. They cover his shin guards. He puts his soccer cleats in his bag. Ready or not, it is time to go. Then he remembers Bradford. He opens his sock drawer. Bradford is usually sleeping in Niles's favorite pair of fuzzy red socks. The socks are empty.

"Niles, let's go!" Mom yells from the kitchen.

"Come on, Niles! I have a game, too!" yells Nora.

Niles sighs. "Bradford, where are you?"

He repeats himself a second time. *"Bradford, where are you?"*

"Niles! Now!" says Mom.

"Coming!" Niles grabs his soccer bag. He looks through it quickly. Bradford is not there. There is no more time to look. It is game time.

As soon as Niles gets into his Mom's car, Bradford *poofs* himself into Niles's soccer bag without anyone seeing him. His face is green. He has been holding his breath from inside the garbage can where he has been hiding. Bradford knows he is banned from games. Niles knows Bradford will do almost anything to not miss a game. The only thing that keeps Bradford away from Niles's games is a promise between two friends. If Niles can't find Bradford before a game, then Bradford can't promise not to be there. Bradford's plan works perfectly—except for the banana peels and yogurt cups stuck to his body. That isn't part of the plan. And the crusts from his peanut butter sandwiches? Gross! *Who would want to eat these crusts?* thinks Bradford. He throws them onto the car floor in the backseat from an opening in the top of Niles's soccer bag.

"Okay, team," says Coach Beth. "Does everyone know your place on the field?"

Everyone shakes their heads *yes*. Niles is playing defense. It is his job to keep the ball away from the goal that is right behind him. Coach Beth calls him a defender. Just like in Star Wars when Luke has to defend the galaxy from the evil Darth Vader, Niles has to defend the goal from the evil River Frogs. They are not *really* evil, but they are the other team. Niles is ready.

The players put their hands together in the middle of a close circle, just like in basketball. On the count of three, they yell *team!*

Niles can hear his parents and Nora cheering from the stands. Nora plays later in the day.

Otis is in the goal box. He looks ready. He keeps running back and forth from one end of the goal box to the other. He wears big gloves. Only the goalie can wear gloves. Only the goalie can use his hands. The gloves make his hands bigger to help keep the ball out of the goal.

"Are you ready, Niles?" asks Scotty from midfield. "Isn't this exciting? I am so excited! Aren't you excited?"

"Scotty!" yells Coach Beth. "Stop talking and pay attention. The game is starting."

Scotty loves to ask questions. Not everyone likes Scotty's questions, though. Niles answers Scotty by shaking his head *yes*. He is ready…or not.

The Clearview 9s win the coin toss before the game. Niles knows right away because Della starts jumping up and down.

"We won! We won!"

That's when Niles knows there might be trouble. Because his bag starts jumping up and down, too. And Niles knows that bags can't jump. He unzips it to see Bradford dancing like he is at a wedding. That dragon can really boogie.

"What are you doing here?" whispers Niles.

Bradford *poofs* behind Niles's water bottle.

"I already saw you," says Niles between clinched teeth.

Bradford *poofs* back. "You know I can't miss your first game, Niles. Plus, you know…" Bradford smiles.

"I know *what?*" asks Niles.

"You know how dreamy that redheaded girl is." If Bradford had eyelashes, they would be fluttering up and down like he was in love.

Niles is mad. First, Bradford came to the game knowing that he was not supposed to be here. Second, Bradford came to the game to see Della, *not* him!

"Stay out of sight!" Niles zips the bag up tight.

Now, all Niles can think about is keeping the soccer ball out of the goal behind him. Rashid is smiling on the other side of the field. He is a forward. He gets to shoot the ball toward the goal. That makes him happy. Really, most things make Rashid happy. Della and Maggie are also forwards.

Connor, Scotty and Lila spread out in the other positions on the field. Nick, Vinnie, Kate, and Kyle sit on the bench.

Since Della won the toss, the Clearview 9s kick first. She stands away from the soccer ball. She takes a running start and kicks the ball with all her might. It goes flying in the air toward the River Frogs' goal. Rashid takes the ball from there. He dribbles it with his feet in between River Frogs. He is fast. Della yells for Rashid to pass the ball to her. But a River Frogs' player gets in the way and tries to steal the ball.

"Rashid!" yells Della again. "You have to be faster!"

And while Della is yelling at Rashid, the River Frogs kick the ball across the center of the field into Niles's territory. Niles follows the ball with his eyes. Lila controls the ball with her feet. She kicks it to Niles. Niles kicks the ball up the field away from the goal and Otis. A River Frogs' player kicks it back toward the goal again. This time Maggie kicks the ball. Lila follows with a hard kick that makes it all the way to Della. Della does not even look for her teammates to pass the ball to. She takes control, dribbles past the River Frogs, and kicks the ball into the goal. The net flutters in the wind as if to congratulate her. But she doesn't need any congratulating. She does that all by herself.

"Yes! Yes! Yes!" she yells. "Take *that,* River Frogs! That's how you play soccer!"

Niles looks to the sidelines while the soccer ball is set in the middle of the field again. Sure enough, his bag is rocking back and forth. Bradford must be doing somersaults in there. That makes Niles so mad that he doesn't realize the other team has kicked the ball. It sails right past him. A River Frogs' player kicks it toward Otis. He dives for the ball. He misses. The score is one-one.

Coach Beth screams at Niles from the sideline. Bradford hears her. Nothing makes Bradford angrier than someone being mean to his best friend. Bradford thinks that Coach Beth is being mean. He also doesn't think clearly when he is mad. Bradford *poofs* out of the soccer bag and drops his special surprise on top of Coach Beth's head when the referee blows the whistle for the kickoff. Bradford *poofs* back into the bag so fast he isn't seen by anyone in the crowd. The next thing the crowd hears is a scream. Followed by another scream. Followed by another scream. Coach Beth jumps up and down on the sidelines, waving her hands over her head. She picks at her head and throws Bradford's special surprise on the field—a cockroach. Big, black, ugly, and active, moving its legs in all directions. She is so loud that the referee blows the whistle to see what the problem is. Niles can guess. He can always guess the reason for a problem—*Bradford*.

The referee sees the cockroach on the field. He picks it up and runs to the garbage can. Coach Beth drinks cup after cup of water to calm down. *She really does not like bugs* thinks Niles and most everyone else in the room.

Bradford smiles from inside the soccer bag. He hopes that Coach Beth will be nicer now. And he's not one bit sad that he won't be having a cockroach for his afternoon snack. That was the only good treat he found in the garbage can.

The River Frogs win the game 3-2. Della scored both of the Clearview 9s' goals. Bradford is so proud. But Niles is angry. He is angry that Coach Beth pulled him out of the game at halftime and never gave him another try. He is angry at

Bradford for making Coach Beth so angry. He is angry he cannot go home after the game because Nora has a game.

Bradford tries to help. He always tries to help. He grabs Niles's wrist when he reaches into the bag for a granola bar. He will not let go.

"Stop it!" Niles says too loud. His Mom looks at him funny. Niles smiles.

"Psst, I need to talk to you. Take me into the hall," says Bradford.

"No," whispers Niles.

Bradford grabs Niles by the wrist even tighter. Dragons are very strong, even little ones. Niles picks up his bag with his other hand and runs out into the hall. Bradford bounces against the inside of the bag. He lets go of Niles.

Niles unzips the bag.

"You didn't have to run so fast," says Bradford. He rubs his head.

"You are always causing trouble," says Niles.

Bradford's eyes flutter. He makes his best sad face. "That coach was not nice," he says.

"It is not her job to be nice. She is trying to teach us things. I was not paying attention. She was teaching me to pay attention." Niles throws his bag to the ground.

"Ouch!" says Bradford. He rubs his head again.

Niles slumps to the floor. No one else is nearby. "You don't have to fight my battles, Bradford. I don't need you at my games."

Bradford scoots to the back of the soccer bag. He turns his head away from Niles. "I was only trying to help." Bradford speaks so softly that Niles does not hear him. Niles zips up the bag. He returns to watch Nora finish her game. He is just in time to see her score the game-winning goal. *Good for her*, thinks Niles. *Good for her.* He sinks down on the bleachers. He doesn't know that his best friend in the world is *poofing* away at that very moment.

Chapter 6:

Niles stays up late talking to Nora. She gives Niles tips on his soccer play. *Watch the ball at all times. Look for your teammates. Pass the ball when you can. Or kick the ball as far up the field as you can away from your goal. Have fun. Don't be so hard on yourself. It's your first year playing.*

When Niles packs his bag the next day for his game, he makes extra sure that Bradford is not inside. He even checks again when he gets to the car. No Bradford. In fact, there hasn't been any sign of Bradford since he left his sister's game yesterday. Niles isn't worried. He doesn't feel like picking a fight with Bradford right now. All he wants to do is to play well in the game.

"You ready to try this position again?" asks Coach Beth. She points to the letter X on her clipboard. The X stands for *defender.*

"I am," says Niles. "I am ready."

"He'd better be ready," says Della. "We lost that last game because of him." She squints her eyes at Niles.

Niles wants to squint right back in her face. But he looks at Rashid instead. Rashid is smiling. Smiling is better than squinting.

"Who are we playing, Coach?" asks Scotty. "Are they good? Do you think we have a chance?"

Coach Beth puts up her hand, "Scotty, take a breath. Focus on yourself. Focus on the

Clearview 9s. The rest you will figure out soon. Hands up!"

"Team!"

The Clearview 9s run onto the soccer field. Otis takes his place in the goal. Della, Kate, and Kyle stand ready to score. Niles, Vinnie, and Lila stand ready to defend their goal. Maggie plays in the midfield. Her job is to help the defenders *and* the forwards. The Kangaroo Kickers win the coin toss. They kick first. This time Niles is ready, though. He defends the goal. He dribbles the ball around a Kangaroo Kicker. He passes the ball to Lila. She passes it back to Niles. He shoots it as hard as he can across the centerline.

"I got it!" yells Della. She kicks the soccer ball. Kate is wide open for a shot at the goal. Della does not see her. Or maybe she does, but she doesn't care. Della dribbles around the Kangaroo Kickers' defenders. She shoots. She scores!

Niles cheers along with the other Clearview 9s. Della puts out her hand for everyone to high five her. They all do. The Kangaroo Kickers don't get to kick off yet because the referee blows the whistle. The half is over. The players meet their coaches on the sidelines.

"Everyone get water," says Coach Beth. "Nice teamwork. Good job on the field."

Della reaches into her bag for her water bottle. "Who has been in my bag?" she yells.

No one answers.

"Who has been in my bag?" she repeats.

"What's the matter, Della?" asks Scotty.

"There are shells all over my bag!"

Niles's eyes get big. *Bradford.* "Did you have peanuts in your bag?" he asks.

"Yes," says Della. "Niles Woodson, did you take my snack?" She gets close to his face, spitting out her words.

"I didn't touch your bag," says Niles.

"Coach Beth, Niles took my peanuts. Niles is lying!"

The referee blows the whistle. The second half is to begin. "Niles, tell Della you are sorry. We have a game to play."

"But, Coach, I didn't touch Della's bag. I didn't touch anything *in* Della's bag."

"She seems to think you did. She must have a good reason why. Sit out this half and think about it. Connor, you play defense for Niles."

Niles sinks to the bleachers. He didn't touch Della's bag before, but he does now. He unzips the bag. He sees peanut shells broken up on the bottom of the bag—definitely Bradford. He reaches his hand all around. Bradford is not there. Niles checks his own bag. Bradford is not there, either. Maybe he spent the night on the soccer field.

The Clearview 9s take the win 3-1. Della scored a second goal. Kate scored the other goal.

Niles can't even celebrate with his team. There is no pleasing Coach Beth—or Della. Niles has never felt so unhappy.

Chapter 7:

Niles spends hours looking for Bradford at home. He looks in all the usual places: his red fuzzy socks in the sock drawer, the bowling ball bag with the red ball, under the bed, and behind the fire engine playset Niles used when he was six. Bradford is nowhere to be found. He needs his best friend. His best friend that annoys him, that causes trouble, his best friend that is his biggest cheerleader. He needs him. He misses him.

Bradford falls to the floor with a thud. He is tired. He was not created to *poof* every half hour. But that is what he must do. Della can't spot him. She might not understand, like Niles. She might not keep him. But he can't go home. Niles is angry. Niles says he ruins everything. Bradford has never felt so unhappy.

Della with the red hair is the girl that makes Bradford's heart beat faster. She isn't fun like Niles, though. She doesn't make him peanut butter sandwiches—no jelly. She doesn't play catch with him. She doesn't teach him things like that tomatoes are also a fruit. She doesn't tuck him into a warm pair of fuzzy socks at night. In fact, all she does is yell at her little brother or brag when she wins a card game. When her dad was left holding the Old Maid card, she ran around the house jumping up and down. Bradford sighs. He misses Niles. But would he want him back?

The doorbell rings. Della's mom answers it. "Della, you have company."

Della runs to the door. Niles, Scotty, and Rashid are standing inside. Rashid smiles. Scotty and Niles wave.

"What are *you* doing here?" she asks.

"Nice to see you, too," says Niles. Rashid steps on Niles's foot, a reminder to play nice.

"Is this your house, Della?" asks Scotty.

Everyone stares at him. "Of course, it's my house. You came here, didn't you?" she says.

Niles takes a deep breath. He reminds himself why he is here. One, try to make peace with Della so she stops causing trouble in the soccer games. Two, try to find Bradford. And bring him home.

"We were hoping you could give us some soccer tips," says Niles.

Her eyebrows shoot up. She looks confused.

"Maybe, you could show us some of your fancy footwork," says Rashid. Everything sounds better when it's coming from Rashid.

"Okay," she says slowly. "We can kick a soccer ball around in the backyard, I guess. Follow me."

Rashid and Scotty follow Della out the back door. Niles holds back.

"I…I need to use the bathroom first," he says.

Della points to a door in the hallway. Niles hears Della's mom and little brother in the basement. He knows this is his best chance to find Bradford. He walks down the hall, looking in bedrooms until he finds the one he thinks belongs to Della. There are soccer trophies and cheerleading ribbons all over the room.

"Bradford," he whispers. "Bradford, are you here? It's me, Niles." Niles looks under the bed. He opens drawers. He looks behind the curtains.

Bradford startles awake. He hears sounds. He is about to *poof* into the back of Della's closet when he hears a voice he knows—*Niles*. He waits.

"Bradford, if you can hear me, I want you to know I am sorry. I am sorry for yelling at you. I know you try to help. Please come home. I miss you. It is not the same without you."

Bradford peeks his head out from under Della's pillow. Niles sees him.

"Hi, buddy," Niles says. He sits down on Della's bed.

Bradford jumps onto the blanket next to him. "Hi, Niles."

"Can you come home with me? I miss you."

"I miss you, too," says Bradford. "I am sorry, too. I didn't try to get you into trouble with that mean coach."

"It's okay. She's just trying to make us better."

"She has a funny way of doing that."

Niles laughs. "I guess you are right about that."

"I learned something interesting," says Bradford.

"What's that?"

"I guess I don't love everything that's red after all."

"Really? What don't you like?"

This time Bradford giggles. "Girls with red hair aren't all as amazing as I thought they were."

"Let's get you home," I say. "I think Mom is making peanut butter sandwiches for dinner."

"No jelly?"

"No jelly, Bradford."

They hear the sliding glass door to the backyard opening. "Niles! Where are you?" It's Della.

"Coming!" yells Niles. He and Bradford jump off the bed too quickly. They knock over a soccer trophy. The trophy knocks into another trophy. That trophy knocks over a display of cheerleading medals.

"Uh-oh!" says Bradford.

"Uh-oh!" says Niles.

Bradford *poofs* into Niles's backpack as Niles runs outside to join his friends and Della for their *lesson*. Niles doesn't care what happens next. He has his best friend back. That is all that matters.

Chapter 8:

The final game of the soccer season is today. Della still brags—a lot, but also says nice things to teammates, too. Ever since Niles, Rashid, and Scotty went to her house, she's been kinder. Well, she did have a fit about her trophies and medals, but Niles said he was sorry. He told her he was amazed at how well she had done to earn all those prizes. That made Della happy right away. Some people just need more noticing than others.

"Niles, I want you to play forward today with Della and Maggie," says Coach Beth. You will be a possible scorer."

"Yes, Coach," says Niles.

"Yes!" says Bradford from inside the soccer bag.

"I am glad you are happy," says Coach Beth. She smiles. That does not happen often. Niles *and* Bradford smile, too.

The Glen Park Bulldogs bring their best skills today. They trap the ball to stop it and kick the direction they want to send it. They dribble and volley the ball with speed.

The Bulldogs kick the ball out of bounds. Niles throws the ball in. He is supposed to keep his feet on the ground when he throws the ball over his head. He forgets. But this time Della and Coach Beth do not yell at him. Instead, Della says, "Try to remember next time."

Bradford does not need to hide from Niles. He has permission to be here—as long as he stays hidden from everyone else. Bradford watches the game from the mesh opening at the end of the soccer bag. He kicks the bag like he is kicking the soccer ball himself. He imagines having a whole team of dragons to play soccer with. But if that can't happen, living with Niles is the next best thing.

"Okay, we have a tied game, boys and girls," says Coach Beth. "Keep the defense tight. Watch where you dribble the ball. Let's get more shots at the goal. That's the way we win! *Team* on three. *One, two, three, team!*"

The game stays tied with two minutes left. Everyone is tired. Everyone on both teams is playing well. Della can't take shots at the goal like she wants to. The Glen Park Bulldogs play good defense when she has the ball. They know how good she is, too.

The clock ticks down. A tie isn't the worst way to end the season. But Della has other ideas. "Niles, run toward the goal!" she yells.

"Why?" he asks, as he runs closer to the goal.

"Stop asking questions like Scotty, and just *run!*"

Niles trips over the ball as it is passed to him, but he recovers and kicks it backwards to

Della who stands in front of the goal. She kicks it back to Niles who is still running toward the goal.

"Score! Score! Score!"

Niles can hear his teammates and Coach Beth chanting from the sidelines. He dribbles past the defender in front of him and gives the ball the hardest kick he can—right into the goal! He also lands on his bottom as his feet go flying out from under him. But he doesn't care. The referee blows the whistle. The game is over. The Clearview 9s are winners.

"Way to stay with the ball, Niles," says Coach Beth. "And, Della?"

"Yes?"

"Nice pass."

They both smile. So, does Niles. And, so does Bradford, who is laying on his stomach in the bottom of the soccer bag. His legs are up in the air. He props up his chest with his elbows on the ground. He eats a peanut butter sandwich with extra spoonfuls of peanut butter—because that's how best friends take care of each other.

Thank you for reading, *Niles and Bradford: Soccer Kicks.* Please consider leaving a review on Amazon. Thank you.

Special thanks to Savanna Tate and Nick Foxworthy for their soccer guidance. Thanks, also, to Chris and Anne, for their first draft recommendations.

Other Children's Books by Marcy Blesy:

Niles and Bradford, Baseball Bully

There are two things that nine-year-old Niles can count on when his family moves to a new town. One, his love for trying new sports will help him meet people. Two, his friendship with his pet dragon Bradford means he will never be alone. However, when a bully on the baseball team makes life hard for Niles, Bradford's idea of helping his friend gets him banned from the game.

Niles and Bradford, Basketball Shots

There are two things that nine-year-old Niles can count on when his family moves to a new town. A sport loving boy and his pet dragon. One, his love for trying new sports will help him meet people. Two, his friendship with his pet dragon Bradford means he will never be alone. However, when things do not go as well as planned during an important basketball game, Niles starts to doubt himself.

Niles and Bradford, Track Team

There are two things that nine-year-old Niles can count on when his family moves to a new town. One, his love for trying new sports will help him meet people. Two, his friendship with his pet dragon Bradford means he will never be alone. However, an unexpected track injury and an unexpected new friend teach him the real meaning of a team.

Evie and the Volunteers Series

Join ten-year-old Evie and her friends as they volunteer all over town meeting lots of cool people and getting into just a little bit of trouble. There is no place left untouched by their presence, and what they get from the people they meet is greater than any amount of money.

Dax and the Destroyers: (a new *Evie and the Volunteers* spin-off featuring a popular character)

Book 1: House Flip

Twelve-year-old Dax spends the summer with his Grandma. When a new family moves into the run-down house across the street, Dax finds a fast friend in their son Harrison. Not to be outdone by his friends, Evie and the Volunteers, and all of their good deeds, Dax finds himself immersed in the business of house flipping as well as Harrison's family drama. But don't expect things to go smoothly when Evie and her friends get word of this new volunteer project. Everyone has an opinion about flipping this house.

Book 2: Park Restoration

Am I Like My Daddy?

Join seven-year-old Grace on her journey through coping with the loss of her father while learning about the different ways that people grieve the loss of a loved one. In the process of learning about who her father was through the eyes of others, she learns about who she is today because of her father's personality and love. Am I Like My Daddy? is a book designed to help children who are coping with the loss of a loved one. Children are encouraged to express through journaling what may be so difficult to express through everyday conversation. Am I Like My Daddy? teaches about loss through reflection.

Am I Like My Daddy? is an important book in the children's grief genre. Many books in this genre deal with the time immediately after a loved one dies. This book focuses on years after the death, when a maturing child is reprocessing his or her grief. New questions

arise in the child's need to fill in those memory gaps.

Be the Vet:

Do you like dogs and cats?

Have you ever thought about being a veterinarian?

Place yourself as the narrator in seven unique stories about dogs and cats. When a medical emergency or illness impacts the pet, you will have the opportunity to diagnose the problem and suggest treatment.

Following each story is the treatment plan offered by Dr. Ed Blesy, a 20-year-practicing veterinarian. You will learn veterinary terms and diagnoses while being entertained with fun, interesting stories.

This is the first book in the BE THE VET series.

For ages 9-12

Be the Vet, Volume 2

What's it Like to Be the Vet?

Made in the USA
San Bernardino, CA
23 February 2020

64870725R00044